The Henry Logan Collection

Moaning Bones

African-American Ghost Stories

Moaning Bones

African-American Ghost Stories

RETOLD BY
JIM HASKINS

WITH ILLUSTRATIONS BY
FELICIA MARSHALL

Lothrop, Lee & Shepard Books ⚊ Morrow
New York

∽ *To Margaret Emily* ∽

Text copyright © 1998 by Jim Haskins
Illustrations copyright © 1998 by Felicia Marshall

Published by Lothrop, Lee & Shepard Books
an imprint of Morrow Junior Books
a division of William Morrow and Company, Inc.
1350 Avenue of the Americas, New York, NY 10019
www.williammorrow.com

Printed in the United States of America.

10   9   8   7   6   5   4   3   2   1

Library of Congress Cataloging-in-Publication Data
Haskins, James, date.
Moaning bones: African-American ghost stories/retold by Jim Haskins;
with illustrations by Felicia Marshall.
p. cm.
Summary: More than fifteen tales from the oral tradition probably
originally recorded in the 1920s and 1930s such as "The Haunted
Stateroom," "Black Tom," and "The Ghost in the Backseat."
ISBN 0-688-16021-2
1. Afro-Americans—Folklore.   2. Tales—United States.   3. Ghost stories.
[1. Afro-Americans—Folklore.   2. Folklore—United States.   3. Ghosts—
Folklore.]   I. Marshall, Felicia, ill.   II. Title.   PZ8.1.H267Mo 1998
398.25'089'96073—dc21   98-14275   CIP   AC

Acknowledgments

The author is grateful to Patricia A. Allen and Deborah Brudno for their help. Special thanks to Kathy Benson.

"The Ghost in the Backseat," a story from Maryland, adapted from "Sudden Disappearance" in Harry Middleton Hyatt, *Hoodoo-Conjuration—Witchcraft—Rootwork: Beliefs Accepted by Many Negroes and White Persons, These Being Orally Recorded Among Blacks and Whites. Memoirs of Alma Egan Hyatt Foundation.* Hannibal, Mo.: Western Publishing Co., 1970–74, p. 31. From the same source: "The Hole They Couldn't Fill," a story from Jacksonville, Florida, adapted from "Bottomless Pit" (p. 35); "Looks Like Jesus," a story from New York City, adapted from "Looked Like Jesus," (p. 30); "The Moaning Bones," another story from Jacksonville, Florida, adapted from a story of the same title (p. 36); "The Haunted Stateroom," a story from Hampton, Virginia, adapted from "Spirit Aboard" (p. 37).

"Big Fraid and Li'l Fraid," adapted from Daryle Dance Cumber, chapter 3, "Dese Bones Gon' Rise Again," in *Shuckin' and Jivin'.* Bloomington: Indiana University Press, 1978, pp. 30–31. From the same source: "'Cinderella' and the Buried Treasure," adapted from "In the Name of the Lord" (p. 34).

"Black Tom," adapted from a story by George S. Schuyler in "Black Art," *American Mercury,* vol. 27 (November 1932), p. 338.

"Find My Child!" adapted from "Fine My Chile," in *Tales of the Congaree,* edited by Robert G. O'Meally, a reissue of Edward C. L. Adams, *Congaree Sketches and Nigger to Nigger,* 1927 and 1928. Chapel Hill: University of North Carolina Press, 1987, p. 68. From the same source: "The Lake of the Dead," adapted from a story of the same title (pp. 32–33); "The Ghost of Gabe," adapted from "The Ghost of White Hall" (pp. 223–25); "The Ghost Owl," adapted from "Transmigration" (pp. 60–61); and "Old Moccasin's Ghost," adapted from a story of the same title (pp. 221–22).

"Old Hy-Ty," adapted from a story of the same title in *Hush, Child! Can't You Hear the Music?* collected by Rose Thompson, edited by Charles Beaumont. Athens: University of Georgia Press, 1982, pp. 65–67.

"The Mysterious Pile of Quilts," adapted from a report in "Ghostlore: The Dead." Reproduced from the original, the Newbell Niles Puckett Collection of the Cleveland Public Library, John G. White Collection.

"The Ghost Yearling," adapted from J. Mason Brewer, *American Negro Folklore*. Chicago: Quadrangle Books, 1968, pp. 60–61.

"You Shot Me Once," adapted from Newbell Niles Puckett, *Folk Beliefs of the Southern Negro*. Montclair, N.J.: Patterson Press, 1926, reprinted by Patterson Smith Publishing Co., 1968, p. 123.

Contents

Introduction

HUSH, CHILDREN. GATHER 'ROUND AND LISTEN. You're about to be scared out of your shoes!

Isn't it fun to shiver and squirm, then laugh at ourselves for being scared by an old ghost story? Today we laugh. But people didn't always laugh at ghost stories. A lot of people really believed in them—and not just African Americans. In fact, just as most African Americans are of mixed African and European blood, African-American ghost stories are usually a combination of African and European folklore. In some instances, the stories could have been handed down among people of just about any heritage who believed in eternal souls and spirit journeys.

The majority of the stories in this book are about the spirits of dead people who for one reason or another could not rest in peace. These spirits, also called dream souls, might go about restlessly because they were not given a proper funeral—in which case they were doomed to wander the face of the earth forever—or because they had left some unfinished business on earth and couldn't rest until they had finished it. Not all are evil; some are even funny.

Most of the stories that follow are based on tales collected in the 1920s and 1930s, when folklorists began to take a scholarly interest in the legends handed down by Americans of all ethnic heritages. Some of the most intriguing were those told by African Americans, perhaps because of their long, long oral tradition that dates back to ancient Africa. We are fortunate today that folklorists collected and saved those legends, because there are not that many good ghost stories told anymore. We are a much more visual society now, and we can go to horror movies and watch TV series based on scary stories. But there's nothing like reading or telling a good ghost story and allowing our imaginations to create spooky pictures in our minds.

Big Fraid and Li'l Fraid

THERE ONCE WAS A LITTLE BOY WHO USED TO GO home through the woods at night all by himself. Most people believed that ghosts prowled those woods, and they couldn't understand how the little boy could travel that way without fear. One day a neighbor asked him, "Boy, aren't you afraid to walk about at night in those dark woods?"

The boy was puzzled. "What is a Fraid?" he asked. "What's it look like? I ain't never seen a Fraid."

The neighbor answered, "Well, you keep traveling through those woods at night, you're going to see a Fraid and he's going to scare you, too."

Now the neighbor had an idea. He would make sure the boy saw a Fraid. He put a sheet over himself and practiced jumping out of the bushes and saying, "Boo!" The neighbor had a monkey for a pet, and the monkey watched what he was doing.

A night or two later, when he saw the boy start out for the woods, the man grabbed his sheet and took out after the boy, circling around so as to get in front of him. He didn't notice that his monkey had grabbed a pillow-case and followed.

The man hid behind a tree deep in the woods and waited for the little boy. When he approached, the man, clad in his sheet, jumped out and said, "Boo!" But at the same moment, the monkey, with the pillowcase over its body, jumped on top of the man!

The man screamed in terror and took off running, with the monkey right behind him and the little boy hollering, "Run, Big Fraid, 'cause Li'l Fraid's gonna catch ya! Run, Big Fraid. Little Fraid will catch ya!"

When the two white-sheeted figures had disappeared, the little boy continued on his way home, pleased to have seen not one but two Fraids.

The Ghost in the Backseat

A MAN WAS DRIVING LATE AT NIGHT ALONG A LONELY road. As he approached a dangerous spot called Dead Man's Curve, he saw a woman standing at the side of the road. She hailed his car, and he stopped.

"Can you give me a ride?" she asked.

"Where are you going?" he wanted to know.

The woman gave an address, and since it was on his way, the man told her to get in the car.

The woman surprised him by opening a rear door and climbing into the backseat.

"You can sit up front with me," the man said.

"No, I'm fine here," the woman replied.

The man thought it strange that the woman preferred the backseat, but he shrugged his shoulders and drove on. He tried to engage her in conversation, but when she didn't reply, he stopped trying and drove on in silence.

Reaching the address the woman had given, the man stopped the car, got out, and opened the back door. He was shocked to see that the backseat was empty. The woman had disappeared! Since he had not made any stops after picking her up, he couldn't figure out what had happened to her.

Disturbed and upset, the man went to the house and rang the doorbell. When he told the man who answered the door about his eerie experience, that man didn't seem surprised at all.

"It was my wife you had in the backseat," he said. "She was killed last winter in an accident at Dead Man's Curve. Quite a few motorists have had the same experience you had."

Black Tom

Black Tom was a conjurer, feared and respected by the simple folk, black and white, for miles around Syracuse, New York. No one had ever seen him do a lick of work, and yet he was always well dressed and had plenty of money in his pocket. Tall and slender, he had black skin and gray eyes and carried a hook-handled cane, the tapping of which could be heard at great distances. No one ever found out where he lived. But while Black Tom might have been feared, he was the one to whom people turned when they needed some serious conjuring done.

On the outskirts of town was a colonial mansion that had belonged to a wealthy gentleman before the Revolutionary War. One winter evening, while a great ball was in progress, Indians had surrounded the place and massacred the family and all the guests, staining the snowdrifts with their blood. No one would live in the mansion after that, and it slowly fell apart. But every year on the anniversary of the slaughter, the old structure was suddenly and mysteriously illuminated, and through the windows passersby could see graceful couples moving back and forth.

The neighboring farmers grew tired of this annual visitation and burned down the house. But all attempts to turn the property into farm-land failed, for nothing would grow there. It was Black Tom who finally threw the spell off, although no one knew how he did it.

In addition to his ability to cast and throw off spells, Black Tom was said to be able to turn himself into a black hound. On moonless nights, he would run across the meadows, howling mournfully, scaring late travelers and causing farmers to bar their doors. Finally, fed up with Black Tom's nighttime wanderings, some farmers decided to catch him. They set a trap at the edge of the woods. Then each night they concealed themselves near the trap and listened, hoping to hear a yelp of pain. One night they were rewarded. Several men went to

the trap to see what they had caught, but when they got there, they found nothing. Not only was there no Black Tom, the trap itself had disappeared!

The next morning, the owner of the trap was found dead in his bed, the jaws of the trap clamped around his neck.

You Shot Me Once

A rich plantation owner wanted to increase his holdings to the east, but the land was owned by a neighbor. The rich man offered to buy the land, but the neighbor refused to sell, and the two got into a heated argument. In a fit of rage, the rich man shot his neighbor.

The neighbor was buried in his family plot, which just happened to be on the border of the rich man's land. Going to and from town on his horse, the rich man was forced to pass that graveyard.

The rich man had an elderly slave who had been with him all his life. The old slave worried that his master was in danger from the spirit of the man he had killed, especially at night.

"Sir, you ought not to go past that graveyard," he warned. "Take the longer route from town."

The master pooh-poohed his old slave's fears.

"Well, then, try to get back home before the moon is full," the old slave pleaded. The master explained that it wasn't always possible.

"Sir, at least load your gun with silver bullets," the old slave said finally. "That's the only way you can shoot a ghost dead."

To avoid being pestered further, the master agreed to use silver bullets.

Every time his master went to town, the old slave worried. He got especially concerned when the hour grew late. One night his master was very late arriving home, and the old slave took up a vigil on the doorstep of the big house.

Suddenly two shots rang out from the direction of the cemetery. His heart in his throat, the old slave strained to see into the dark. Not long afterward, he heard the sound of galloping hoofs, and into the front yard came his master's horse, the master himself lying limply across its back.

The old slave helped his master off the horse and got him into the house. When he had recovered enough to speak, the master reported that a ghostly form had seized his horse's bridle. He had drawn his gun and shot at the form twice. But the ghost had merely croaked, "You shot me once; I can't be shot again!" The master couldn't remember what had happened after that. He awoke to find himself being helped from his horse by his faithful servant.

The next morning, the old slave went to the cemetery. There on the road that wound around the graveyard, he found his master's revolver with two cartridges discharged. Shaking his head, he wondered what kind of ghost could be immune to silver bullets.

"Cinderella" and the Buried Treasure

There was once a little orphan girl who was taken in by a local couple after her parents died. But instead of treating her like their own, the couple made her work all day like some kind of Cinderella.

At night, when supper was over, the little girl had to fill a pan with water and wash the dishes on the back porch. This was her least favorite job, because there was something in the shadows that scared her. Every time she went out there to wash the dishes, something frightened her and sent her running back into the house. But the couple just laughed and ordered her back out. Night after night, she went onto that back porch, got scared, ran back in, and got sent back out, until she finally finished the dishes.

But after a time, the couple began to wonder if indeed there was something out there in the night, and they told the preacher about it. "It could be that the child does see something," he said. "I'll come over some evening and sit."

So one night the preacher came to supper. When the meal was over, the little girl went out to the back porch to do the dishes. Sure enough, she soon screamed and came running back into the house.

"Now look, daughter, don't get scared now," the preacher said to her. "Whatever it is, when it comes back again, you say, 'In the name of the Lord, what do you want?' You say, 'Either speak or leave me alone.'"

So the girl went back out into the night, and the thing appeared again. As instructed, she said, "In the name of the Lord, what do you want?"

The thing replied, "Take a pick and shovel and follow me."

So the girl found a pick and shovel and followed the thing. It led her across the moonlit yard, into the woods, and down into a little valley. Then it stopped by a large tree and said, "You dig right here by this tree, and you'll find

a big earthen jar full of gold coins. Now some of that money's gonna spill out when you dig it up, and I'm gonna tell you who I want you to give it to. But what stays in that jar will be yours."

Well, the girl started digging, and she found the jar. And when she pulled the jar out of the ground, some of the coins spilled out. The ghost told her who to give the money to, and she did as she was told. But the rest was hers.

Now that the little girl was rich, the couple who had taken her in started treating her real good. She didn't have to work anymore.

And the ghost never came back.

The Ghost Yearling

Two men used to pass an old barn on the nights they went into town. The barn was rickety and falling apart, and they didn't think much about it. Then one night as they passed by, they saw a yearling calf standing outside. She wasn't tethered; she just stood there.

"That's one fine calf," said Gibbie, one of the men. "Wonder where she came from."

The next night they passed by, the calf was still there, as she was the next, and the next. Weeks later, the calf was still standing there. Strangely, she did not seem to grow any larger.

At last Gibbie made up his mind. If the yearling was still there the next time they passed the barn, he was going to take her home.

A few nights later they went to town, and sure enough, the calf was still there by the old barn. Gibbie went up to her and took her by the ears. The calf pulled and twisted, so Gibbie jumped on her back and tried to hold her.

The calf jumped higher. "Hold her, Gibbie!" shouted his friend.

"I got her!" answered Gibbie, holding on tight.

But the calf kept on jumping. She jumped higher and higher until she was nearly out of sight.

"Hold her, Gibbie!" shouted the other man, straining his eyes to see his friend and the calf.

"I got her, or she got me!" shouted Gibbie, as he disappeared from view.

And that was the last time anyone ever saw either Gibbie or the calf.

Find My Child!

"Brother, don't ever cross over Barrs Field," Paul told Jimmy.

"Why not?" asked Jimmy.

"Well," Paul began, "one day, I was going from Dry Branch to Pea Ridge, and when I started across Barrs Field, I saw a little woman. She was wearing a checked gingham dress and a red handkerchief around her head, and she had a bunch of keys hanging from her apron. She came up right in front of me, and I said hello. She didn't say hello back, just 'Where's my child?' And she looked at me, and she didn't look natural, and I started walking, and she walked beside me. She asked again, 'Where's my child?'

"I started walking faster, and she walked faster. I started to run, and she ran. I turned off Pea Ridge Crossing, and she rose up in front of

me, and she didn't touch the ground. 'Find my child!' she said, and she floated off into the air.

"And even after she was gone, I heard her moaning—in the bushes, in the fields, in the sky, in the clouds—'Where's my child? Find my child.'

"It wasn't life and it wasn't death, and it wasn't natural. My ears were bursting and my head was full, and I couldn't hear anything but the moaning of that woman—'Where's my child? Find my child.'"

Jimmy shivered. "I bet you never went back to Barrs Field."

"That's the fastest way to get home," said Paul. "I cross over there all the time, and that woman is always there. On dark nights and moonlit nights, this woman walks. She isn't a woman, she's a restless spirit, and she walks from Pea Ridge to Dry Branch. She's always moaning, and the sound of her voice mixes up with the rattle of her keys and the swish of her dress. The light of her eyes can be seen on the earth, and the sound of her voice can be heard in the skies and in the dark bushes and in the air, over the fields and across the woods, from Pea Ridge to Dry Branch: 'Where's my child? Find my child.'"

The Ghost of Gabe

Back in slavery times, a slave named Gabe lived on the White Hall plantation. He had restless ways and made people uneasy, but they were sort of used to him. Then one day he disappeared, and no one knew what had happened to him.

Years later, Gabe came back. He emerged from the woods late one evening, and met up with an old man named Long Jim. It was a cold, cold night, and Long Jim was just about frozen. He said to Gabe, "Let's find some shelter. No one lives in the White Hall house now; all the folks have gone away."

So Gabe and Long Jim went to the White Hall house. They collected some wood and built a fire in the fireplace. Long Jim sat by the fire and looked around, and he started getting a creepy feeling.

Every time the wind whistled, the old house trembled and cracked and groaned, and Long Jim started imagining people coming out from the shadows. He thought of the white folks who used to live in the house, and of the slaves who worked there. Several times he thought he recognized faces in a window, and when he saw the faces the shutters rumbled and rolled.

To get his mind off what he thought he was seeing, Long Jim tried to talk to Gabe. But Gabe wasn't in a talking mood.

Suddenly, Long Jim heard a voice out in the wind calling, "Gabe, Gabe." The voice rose to a scream: "Gabe, Gabe!" Then it turned into a wail: "Gabe, Gabe, Gabe!"

Long Jim looked at Gabe, and Gabe laughed. It wasn't exactly a laugh, more like a cackle, as if he was trying to aggravate the voice that was calling to him.

The voice came closer and closer, and the sound was dreadful to Long Jim's ears. Gabe just got up, stretched as if he was tired, and walked out.

Long Jim had no idea where Gabe had gone, but he was afraid to be alone by the fire. He went into a dark corner and sat on a box, but

he had barely sat down when the door opened. A tall man walked into the room carrying a potato sack. He threw the sack on the floor by the fire, and whatever was in it clanked as the sack fell.

Then the tall man opened the sack and dumped its contents on the floor, and Long Jim could see that it was a pile of bones. Arm bones and foot bones and hand bones and back bones.

Working on the floor in front of the fire, the tall man joined the bones together until he had produced the full skeleton of a man. Then he looked down at the skeleton and laughed, grabbed it by the hand, and lifted it up. Putting one arm around the skeleton's waist, he started to dance with it. And Long Jim realized that the skeleton was Gabe.

The Ghost Owl

A man was crossing the big swamp when he decided he was too tired to go on and had to rest. So he lay down with his head on a log and soon dropped off to sleep.

After a while, he heard someone laughing and talking. Opening one eye, he saw an owl sitting on the stump of a limb on the log. The owl looked down at him and, laughing, asked, "Brother, are you resting?"

"I've been resting, but I'm done with rest now," the man replied. "I'm leaving here."

"Brother, hold on a minute," said the owl. And the man saw that he wasn't really an owl, but the spirit of some person.

The man was even more intent on leaving, but he saw that the owl looked kind of ill and weak, and then he realized the owl was the spirit of his grandfather's friend way back in slavery times. The owl wanted to talk, so the man decided to listen.

The owl complained that he didn't get any rest. He spent his time flying around at night— he couldn't stand the light of day—and talking, most of the time with other spirits, but sometimes he made himself known to humans. He said he hadn't lived right in this world, and his main pleasure was meeting the children of his old friends when they passed out of this world and took on new shapes as he had. He said some of them took on the shapes of different birds and animals, but one shape didn't recognize anybody in a different shape. He said he didn't know when he caught a bird or a snake if he was eating a friend or not. Every time the owl said something like that, he'd laugh, and the man would break out in a cold sweat.

The owl told the man he was going to look for him in his world a little later, and that they would have some good laughing and talking. And then the owl said, "Son, I'm going to put something in your ear you will always remember."

"What is it?" the man wanted to know.

"I can't say it loud," said the owl. "I gotta

whisper it to you." Then he hopped down off the stump and started toward the man, laughing like crazy.

That's when the man decided he'd had enough. He didn't want any spirit world sign, and he didn't want any old men whispering in his ear—especially old dead men. He broke and ran. And the owl floated along behind him, laughing and hollering and making the worst sounds the man had ever heard in his life.

From then on, the man avoided the swamp at night, and he wasn't much for visiting it in the daytime either.

The Haunted Stateroom

In the nineteenth century, before cars were common, many people traveled by steamship. The Old Dominion Lines was a major steamship company operating along the East Coast. One route took passengers between Virginia and Massachusetts, and one of the ships on that route was the *Jamestown*. The *Jamestown* was caught in a big storm around Boston Light one night, and two passengers died, though the *Jamestown* itself suffered only minor damage and was soon repaired.

Several trips later, a young steward aboard the *Jamestown* was ushering passengers to their staterooms. He was carrying a passenger's bags, leading the way to his room, when the passenger stopped to talk to another passenger. The boy continued on to the room, unlocked the door, and placed the bags inside. Then he locked the door, but he left the key in the lock so the passenger could let himself in.

The passenger finished his conversation and went to his stateroom. But when he got to the room, he found the door locked and the key gone. Angrily, he called for the steward, the porter, and the conductor, and demanded his key. But no one knew where it was. Everyone accused the young steward of taking it, but he protested his innocence.

The chief engineer was called to pry open the door. When he did so, the onlookers were shocked to see the room in total disarray. The baggage was scattered all over the place. The beds were all rumpled. The room looked as if a storm had hit it.

Then the employees of the ship remembered that it was in that very stateroom on the *Jamestown* that the two passengers had died during the storm off Boston Light. The ghosts of those dead passengers had returned.

The Hole They Couldn't Fill

A man who was a night watchman in the railroad yards was killed by a train one night. Some said he must have fallen in front of the train by accident, but his mother suspected that the night switchman had pushed her son in front of an oncoming train. The suspect had been in jail before, and she knew there had been bad blood between him and her son.

The woman prayed to her son every night, asking how she could help him get back at his killer. At last, it came to her what she could do.

The next night, she went to the graveyard where her son was buried. At the head of his grave, she dug a small hole. Then she put her hands into the hole and prayed for her son to return to haunt his killer.

Meanwhile, over in the railroad yard, the night switchman mysteriously fell asleep on

SONNY JOHNSON

UNEXPLAINED DEATH

the switch. With no one to switch the tracks, trains coming through the station nearly bumped into one another.

The following morning, the man awakened with no recollection of what had happened.

The next night it rained, and the woman decided to stay inside rather than visit her son's grave. Over at the rail yard, the switchman stayed awake all night, and there was no danger of accidents.

But the following night was clear and dry, and the woman again went to the graveyard, dug a hole at the head of her son's grave, and pushed her hands deep down into the earth. Over at the rail yard, the switchman, who was walking along the track, suddenly fell into a deep hole.

The next morning, the day workers arrived at the rail yard to find that the night switchman had disappeared. All they saw was a big deep hole, and his lantern lying next to it.

They tried to fill up the hole, but it wouldn't close. And ever since, whenever the weather is dry, people hear the missing night switchman hollering. On rainy nights he's silent, but on dry nights he makes a real racket.*

*This story is said to refer to the bottomless pit mentioned in the Bible, in Revelation 9:11, 11:7, 17:8, 20:1 and 3.

Looks like Jesus

Seven-year-old Lucy lived with her family on a small farm not far from their closest neighbors, the Kanes. The Kanes had a daughter, Mary, who was about Lucy's age. They also had a new baby, and every chance she got, Lucy went to the Kanes's house to visit the baby. One evening she rocked the baby to sleep, then went outside to play with Mary.

It was summertime, and the moon was shining as bright as day. The two little girls could see all the way across the field to the wood, and over to the barn, which was some distance from the house. Suddenly Lucy saw a bright spot near the barn. "Oh, look, Mary!" she cried. "What's coming?"

Mary saw it too. "Oh, Lucy, what is that?"

"I don't know," said Lucy. "It looks like Jesus."

The apparition was a tall man with long

hair, wearing a long white robe. The bottom of the robe wasn't touching the ground. As the girls watched, the ghost rose higher and higher, making an arc from where the sun rose in the morning to where it set in the evening.

Frightened, the girls ran into the kitchen, where Mary's mother was baking bread. "What is the matter with you?" she asked as they stumbled into the kitchen hollering.

The girls told her what they had seen, but she didn't believe them. "You didn't see anything," she said. "It's just the glow of the lamp sitting in the window."

But Lucy and Mary knew what they had seen. They went out the next night, and the next, trying to find that mysterious apparition. But they never saw it again.

Old Hy-Ty

There was once a very tall man, tall as a tower. He got into trouble with some folks, and they killed him. Then they put his body back on his horse and rode him out of town. He has been traveling ever since, because if you don't die happy, you are doomed to stay on the road.

The ghost of this very tall man was so active for a time that everyone around knew about him. They called him Hy-Ty.

Hy-Ty was not an especially frightening haunt. He presented himself night and day, but mostly he seemed to mind his own business. One night someone saw him sitting astride a small roadhouse, one leg on each side of the roof, not bothering anybody.

There was one time, however, when he scared a man half to death. It was Sunday morning, and the man decided to climb a tree

and frighten the womenfolk as they passed by on their way to church. He was up in the tree, waiting, when old Hy-Ty came along. Old Hy-Ty was so tall that his head reached way up into the tree where the man was hiding, and the sight of Hy-Ty's big head scared him so much that he fell out of the tree and broke nearly every rib in his body.

According to the local folks, once cars became common and the roads started filling up with them, Hy-Ty didn't go on the roads much. Said one, "Reckon he is scared he will get run over with his old long self."

The Lake of the Dead

There is a lot of swampland on the coast of
South Carolina. The big swamps are filled with
strange creatures and plants, and locals assert
that people are drawn to them "like a trap
draws flies." There is something about the mysterious nature of the swamps that breeds stories of the supernatural, and children on the
South Carolina coast hear them from the
grown-ups and repeat them to one another.

One night Tommy and his younger brother,
Hale, were out hunting possum and not having
much luck. "Something must be dead around
here," said Hale. "See that buzzard up there?
Maybe if we follow it, we can grab whatever it
is that's dead."

They both looked up to watch the buzzard
flying in the light of the moon.

"Stay away from the path of the buzzard,"
Tommy warned Hale, "for if you walk in a buz-

zard's path and you wander too far, you'll land on the shores of the Lake of the Dead."

"What's the Lake of the Dead?" Hale asked, his eyes wide.

"It's a place in that big swamp over yonder," Tommy answered. "Hardly anyone knows where it is, but if you wander far enough and long enough, you find it."

"How do you know about it?" Hale wanted to know.

"I been there," Tommy assured him.

"You lying," said Hale.

"No, I'm not," said Tommy.

"Then let's follow that old buzzard, and you can show me."

The two brothers walked through the swamp for what seemed like hours, following the buzzard by the light of the full moon. At last, the buzzard began to circle in place, and soon the boys entered a clearing and beheld a large lake. The shores were littered with dead things—a hog one place, a cow another, a little bird here, a rabbit there.

As the boys looked around at the body-littered shore, a deer approached from the swampy woods. The animal walked to the edge of the water. It raised its head as if listening intently. Then it stretched its neck out over the water. Suddenly it drew back, then turned tail and ran back into the woods.

"We coulda bagged that deer," Tommy whispered.

"Maybe we should take one of those dead ones," Hale suggested.

"You kidding?" said Tommy. "Even the buzzards aren't eating them."

The boys watched three buzzards walking slowly around the shores of the lake, as if their only purpose was to make the place look more dreadful. They didn't touch the carcasses, just walked around. Once in a while, they shook themselves, stretched out their necks, and made high screeching sounds that made the boys shiver in fright.

"Let's get outta here," whispered Tommy. "I feel like there's another world creeping up on me."

"Is this how you felt the last time?" Hale wanted to know.

"There wasn't any last time. Let's go!" And Tommy took off for the edge of the clearing and the swampy woods.

After they got back home, the boys had a hard time explaining to their folks how they could be out most all night and come back empty-handed. They were too frightened to say where they had been. Their parents noticed afterward that the boys didn't act like themselves anymore. The least little thing scared them. And every time they saw a buzzard circling in the sky, they ran and hid.

The Moaning Bones

There was once a very poor family who eked out a living by scavenging for junk, which they sold to the local junk man. The two boys in the family helped out as much as they could. They spent their days picking up rags, iron, bits of tin, glass bottles, and even the silver paper from cigarette packages. They also picked up bones, for the junk man would pay a penny for a bag of bones.

Not far away from where they lived, there had once been a cemetery. But it had been relocated to a different area. Everyone thought that all the bodies had been dug up and moved to the new spot. But one of the boys in the family discovered otherwise.

The boy had no idea that the field where he found some bones had been a cemetery. All he knew was that he had discovered a treasure trove, and now he could get lots of bones in one place and not have to walk all over town collecting junk.

Naturally, his brother wanted to know where he was getting the bones, but the boy wanted to keep his secret to himself. So he decided to go to the bone field only at night, when his family was sleeping.

One night he went to the old cemetery and filled up a potato sack with bones. Returning home, he tiptoed past his sleeping brother, intending to hide the bones under their bed. But the brother stirred, and the boy feared he might wake him up. So he silently entered his parents' room and hid the sack of bones under their bed instead. Then he crawled into bed beside his brother and fell into a deep sleep.

Around midnight, his parents were awakened by moaning and groaning. The eerie sounds seemed to be coming from under their bed, so the father looked and found the potato sack. He pulled it out and shook its contents onto the floor. The bones moaned even louder.

"These are human bones!" the father exclaimed. He quickly replaced them in the sack, tied it up, and threw it out the window.

The next morning, the boy had some explaining to do. Threatened with a whipping, he told his father where he had found the bones.

"Boy," warned his father, "don't ever bring those bones into the house. That field used to be a burying ground!"

Old Moccasin's Ghost

"Old Moccasin appeared to me the other night," said Tad matter-of-factly.

"Old Moccasin's been dead quite a while," said Tad's friend. "Did you have a talk with him?"

"Did I have a talk with him?" Tad repeated. "I didn't have anything *but* talk, and some of it was mighty frightening.

"When he came, I was lying on my bed resting, and the moon was shining through the window as bright as day. Suddenly I got a feeling that I wasn't alone. 'Who's that?' I said.

"And I heard a voice say, 'I sure am glad to be here one more time.'

"He seemed to be a lot gladder than I was. It doesn't matter how well I knew a man—how close a friend he was to me—when he's dead, I want him to stay dead. I don't want his spirit hanging around my house, breaking my night's rest and telling me all kinds of tales about hell and the devil and different dead people I used to know.

"But I listened to him, and he had some interesting things to say. He said there's all different kinds of places in hell. There's the fiery places, but there's also pastures where the devil sends the people to cool off a bit. He said it would surprise me to know how many different people the devil has in hell. He said he saw a heap of people he knew. And when he left, he pretty much made me feel like there's no use struggling anymore, that most everybody that dies goes to hell, and heaven isn't anything but a great wilderness."

"I'm not sure," said the friend, "but I have a feeling Old Moccasin left you with the right impression."

The Mysterious Pile of Quilts

A WOMAN FELL ILL AND WENT TO LIVE WITH HER brother and his wife so they could take care of her. They let her have their bedroom, while they slept on the couch. The woman spent her last days in that bedroom, sitting in a rocking chair and making quilts, sewing odd scraps of fabric together in various designs.

After the woman died, her brother and his wife moved back into their bedroom. Instead of putting the quilts away in a closet, they piled them on the same chair where the woman had spent so many hours sewing.

But the quilts would not stay on the chair. Every morning when the couple got up, the quilts were on the floor. Since there wasn't anyone in the house but them, they knew something strange was going on. One night, the man decided to try to stay awake and find out.

He was just about to doze off when he heard the quilts hit the floor. He sat up in bed, but all he could see was the chair rocking slowly back and forth, the way his sister used to rock. He reached for the gun he kept by his bed, and just as he did so, he felt a puff of air go past him and out the window into the yard. Just then, the yard dogs started barking.

The man ran out of the house and into the yard. He couldn't see what the dogs were barking at, but he shot in the direction they were looking.

Whatever it was, it didn't come back, and the quilts never fell off the chair again.

About the Author

JIM HASKINS IS THE AUTHOR OF MORE THAN A HUNDRED books for both adults and children, including *The Cotton Club,* which inspired the motion picture of the same name, and *The Story of Stevie Wonder,* which won the Coretta Scott King Award. He was honored with the *Washington Post*/Children's Book Guild Award for the body of his work, and two of his books—*Black Music in America* and *The March on Washington*—won the Carter G. Woodson Award.

Mr. Haskins is currently working on a seven-book series that presents American history from an African-American viewpoint. The first title in the series, *African Beginnings,* was recently published.

He lives in New York City and Gainesville, Florida.